BRIDE OF THE LIVING CHAD

DAMIEN CASEY

Encyclopocalypse Publications
www.encyclopocalypse.com

Bride of the Living Chad

ISBN: 978-1-966037-11-8

Cover Design by Miss Viscera (www.missviscera.etsy.com)
Additional Cover Formatting by Sean Duregger
Interior design and formatting by Sean Duregger
Edited by Candace Nola

BRIDE OF THE LIVING CHAD

THE DAY I FOUND OUT ALL ABOUT LENA WHITE, AND THEN SHE DIED IN A CAR WRECK AND I WAS PRETTY PISSED OFF FOR AN HOUR.

Let me tell you about when I met the love of my life.

I found Lena White on Twitter. Someone commented a GIF of her getting absolutely fucking railed by some dude under a post from the Miami Dolphins about their sixty-point loss to The Patriots.

Brady wasn't even playing.

The Dolphins fucking suck, bruh.

I commented "what's the @?"

Some smart ass tagged an @ and when I clicked on it, there were a bunch of pictures of giant globs of shit in a toilet. The bio said, "caught you slippin'."

Whatever the fuck that means.

I was just trying to find out who the fucking chick was because I had a little spare time before class, and she looked like a fucking pro.

Huge tits.

Blonde hair.

Tanned and firm body with that classic little heart tattoo on her hip.

Goddamn, there was something about the way she looked at the camera, though that did it for me.

Luckily, some other fucking keyboard cowboy posted her real @.

Found it.

Looked her up on the hub.

I had another fifteen minutes before class.

She was fucking great, the body movements, the way she talked to the dude railing her, the fucking way she looked at the camera.

New favorite.

Thank you, weird, perverted guy who keeps porn GIFs on his phone and posts them under NFL team tweets that kids may see.

I question your judgement and think you should be in jail.

But I appreciate what you've done for me on this day.

Three days later my "what's the @" tweet got a response that said, "dun matter bitch she died 2day" with a link to an article about a car wreck featuring a limousine and a Hummer.

Apparently, a crew of pornstars were filming in a

limo when one of them decided to get out of the skylight and flash the passing Las Vegas traffic.

This hella buff dude in a Hummer seen those glorious breasts and couldn't take his eyes off them.

You know that myth that if you stare at the headlights of oncoming traffic, you'll drive into them?

Me and my boys used to try that shit sometimes. It didn't work. We'd all be wildin' and yelling "ah shit son! Here it is! We gonna die!"

No one ever died.

Hummer dude even lived to tell the tale of the limo that blew up after he hit it head on for some reason.

I dunno.

Maybe they had a shit ton of like oils and lube in there for all the sexing and then someone was smoking a blunt and the impact lit the shit on fire?

Who can really say?

But she was dead.

I didn't even know if I could watch her back catalogue because is it even ok to get all bricked up and choke one out to a dead chick?

The mysteries of life abound.

It was when I was really starting to think about all the karmic implications of this shit that I overheard my dickhead bitch boy goth roommate talking on the phone about some shit spell or other Harry Potter shit he learned to reanimate a corpse.

I stood up and got in his face and said, "listen, you little fucking bitch. You're going to show me how to do this fucking spell. I want to bring dead people back to life."

He asked me why, and I told him it was so I could have an undead legion of the hottest bitches on Earth to look at every day.

He asked about decomposition, and I slapped him hard across the face.

Fucking dweeb and his fucking words.

He took me to the library where some weird annoying fucking girl in glasses said she recognized me from Comp two and she really thought my paper about Dugong's being endangered was very heartfelt and informative.

I smiled at her and said thanks; I wanted to ask her if she thought just because I spend most of my time at Drinx and the gym if she thought I was some sort of fucking meathead who didn't appreciate the intricacies of endangered sea life.

But I thought, fuck it. I'm here for a business degree, not to be a marine biologist like this fucking chick, apparently.

I turned around to check her out really quick before I left. I could maybe get my little goodong in some strange thanks to my paper about the Dugong if I tried.

Nah.

Fuck that, I thought.

She had a thick ass sweater on, her tits barely made lumps in it.

Her hips were hella big, too.

Bright ass red hair and those weirdo eyes that looked like a Pixar movie.

Don't get me wrong, I like that on some chicks, but it's got to match all over you know? Not be all dispropor- tionate like a pear.

Anyway, got my fucking book and bounced.

CHAPTER 2
STANDING AROUND COVERED IN HOT SAUCE ASKING WHAT THE FUCK WAS ALL THAT THEN?

First attempt sucked ass.

Second attempt sucked ass.

Third attempt sucked ass.

All these spells were stupid AF.

They were supposed to reanimate Lena and have her firm and bouncy undead ass walking all the way to me.

I know, I know, I know, I'm in Ohio, and she's out in Vegas, I think?

Helluva walk.

The book said she would do a "ghostly jog" or something.

Put me in the mind of when two magnets slap together. Only, she's running full speed ahead through trees and shit to get to me.

I had a girlfriend who was like that in high school.

I'd call, and she'd show up.

Her friends told her I was manipulating her for sex because my other girlfriend at the time wouldn't sleep with me.

I mean, were they right? Absolutely.

But was it cool to be in my business like that? No.

The first spell called for human toenails mixed with freshly cut blades of grass. I went outside with a pair of scissors and went snip, snip, then came in and did the same to my roommate's big toes.

He tried to get pissed, but I think he could see the look of determination in my eyes and decided it would be better to avoid finding out after fucking around.

I said the words; the spell said I would hear her voice call out to me.

I had to print off a picture of her at the library, so the spell knew who it was. That fucking red head looked at it and smirked, like she was laughing at me for printing of five pictures.

"We have campus wide Wi-Fi, you know?"

Can you believe she said that shit?

Like I was some old grandpa about to flog the bishop to low resolution face pics I got from Google images.

"Yeah," I said. "You would fucking know, wouldn't you?"

"Yeah, they basically have it posted on every wall. Everyone knows, my guy."

"I'm not your guy. Never will be."

"Ok…"

"No matter how much you liked my essay about Dugongs."

"I don't get the hostility that's going on here. Ok, maybe I started it. I was just teasing you, though."

"Keep your teases in your back pocket."

Fucking showed her.

I squeezed my ass muscles hard when I left. I knew she was looking. She had to be. Who wouldn't be?

Some fucking marine biologist she was going to turn out to be.

The second attempt needed the picture and boiling water. I printed a bikini pic for this one because I am one clever motherfucker.

The picture just sort of sunk.

I stirred it around a bit.

Again, I was supposed to hear a noise, but I didn't hear shit.

I took the picture out and used the water to make mac and cheese for my roommate.

Marty is alright, but I do enjoy watching him think I'm being nice when in reality I know for a fact I'm only giving him the Three Musketeers bar because I dropped it in the toilet, I was pissing in.

He chomped down on the macaroni and thanked me. He said he was getting so busy with school and Melinda he forgot to eat.

Melinda is his big titty goth girlfriend.

Massive jugs.

They don't look saggy either, I'm always confused about that. I told him they could stay the night here if they wanted. I figured I may get a peek then.

They thanked me and continued to stay at her off-campus apartment.

That's ok.

I would live to fight another day.

The third called for the picture to be soaked in hot sauce and put in the freezer.

Again, no voice.

I double checked that one because that seemed a little fucking fishy to me.

I used the wrong spell; that one was to make someone stay away from you, freeze them, it said.

I ripped the freezer open, and the bag fell out of the shelf. When I tried to grab it, the fucking thing burst and went everywhere.

Then I was back at the fucking library saying, "don't ask," to the marine biologist.

I asked if she knew about any spooky hocus pocus shit.

She said she loved the new one, and they actually had the sequel in the library!

GASP!

I did not give a fuck!

I explained I needed a spell to bring the dead back to life… for, like… my dog…

She felt bad because I used my doe eyes and really laid it on that I loved my fucking dog.

I never had a dog.

My mom is allergic.

She took me to this dusty room, cobwebs everywhere. Gnarly looking dungeon place.

"Here you go," she said. "This one is probably right up your alley."

Ritual Magic for the Capitalist Mind.

I flipped the pages and there it was:was summon this lesser demon, give him a five hundo, he does the job. Now we're talking.

I texted my mom and asked for five hundred bucks.

She Venmo'd it over.

I stood in the mirror and said this guy's name five times while holding out my phone, showing my account balance.

"Mark. Mark. Mark. Mark. Mark."

CHAPTER 3
FUCKIN' MARK RIPPED ME OFF!

"Make it quick, bro. We're playing this one fast and loose. Right to the bones. On a need to know or no basis. There's no truth butt reality. Butt with two T's, you feel me?"

I didn't feel him.

I honestly thought about beating his little ass.

He stood at about four-foot, skin and bones looking dude in a three X shirt.

I swear to God he had glitter in his hair and eyebrows.

"Ok, Mark," I said. "I got your cash."

"Venmo them shits over to me and tell me who you want to be all George Romero Dawn of the Dead, the original, not the remake. You catching this cutie?"

He pointed to a Barbie doll sitting on my desk typing on a typewriter.

"Writings a little hard to read because it's so small, but she comes at a very affordable price. Now, she is a lesbian, so don't try to make a pass at her or anything. Plus, she's a toy I brought to life so I could give her money and tell people I had a secretary. So, she doesn't really have any, like, organs or anything. She can't even move her lips or talk; she just writes shit. She just usually leaves the money lying wherever I hand it to her, too. She's really just a - HEY, MOTHER FUCKER THESE ARE MY SECRETS NOT YOURS."

"Listen, bro. I don't give a shit. Tell me your Venmo, bring Lena White back to life, and then have her here. I would really recommend you be on your way after that."

"Damn... you're the fiftieth request I've had for her... maybe the only one who could put up the cash though... she's a total- well, WAS a total babe. I got it figured she's all burnt up like a crispy chicken sandwich that's been left in the air fryer too long at this point."

"Venmo?" I swear I was going to fuck this guy up. Why wouldn't he just do his job?

"Chill, chill, chill. Alright. Its Mark is the fucking coolest. All one word."

"Mark is a hella normal name for a genie or whatever the fuck you are."

"I hear that a lot! It's not my name. It's just what I use for this because you and every other fucking goober that gives me this money are Marks. You know, like the pro wrestling insider term that the fans use all the time now?"

"No."

"Oh well. Fuck it. She'll be here in a bit."

A knock on the door.

"Looks like she's here now! Gotta run, bro. There's a kid in England who wants his mom brought back. She was sucked up into the engine of an airplane, so I may just buy the kid some red confetti."

I was fucking confused as could be about what he was talking about. Confetti? Why was he implying the kid's mom would still be all chopped up?

Then I opened the door...

CHAPTER 4
ALL OF A SUDDEN I'M LESS INTERESTED

What stood before me looked like someone left their marshmallow over the fire for too long. That happens a lot, right? Like we've come so far as a society I can find someone I went to in fifth grade on the internet, but we can't have a marshmallow cooking app? I used to have this idea for an app that was a chicken sandwich meet up. Basically, you log into this app and it's a giant chatroom. You say where you're eating the chicken sandwich, and others talk to you about it while they eat theirs.

I was typing about how Lena looked before I gave you that award-winning idea; you're welcome, by the way. She was all charred in places with a weird, cooked meat look in others. Her hair was a burnt mess of dry straw. Her one eyelid was sealed shut, presumably from the fire. Her other eye was all glassy, presumably from being dead as shit.

Her tits still looked great, though, not gonna lie.

"Are you Tanner Henry?" she asked.

"Uh... yeah?"

"I want to make a joke about you having two first names, but it looks like my appearance has already been hard enough on you."

She pushed past me and came in. She sat down on Marty's bed and sort of bounced. "This is SO much nicer than that casket I was in," she said. "Or was it a coffin? There's a difference, right? Like one is a rectangle, and the other has that shape?"

I just stared.

Why was she acting like this was a normal, everyday occurrence?

"Jesus," she said. "You didn't think that when you ripped my soul from the afterlife and put it in this body via Venmo spell, that I would look the same, didya?"

"I... um..." I stuttered.

I just kept staring at her tits.

I made eye contact with them like it was the most important thing in the world.

For whatever reason, they didn't seem to get burnt as badly.

She rolled her eyes and stuck her hand into the skin of her lefty.

She pulled out a gelatinous mound and threw it at me.

Her tit went flat, and she said, "now you can play with it as much as you want and quit staring. When the blast happened it pushed me forward, that's why my chest and stomach are moderately ok. I told Peter not to use that much oil. You know what? Do you have a phone handy?"

I pulled out my phone and handed it to her. She brushed it away and said, "Google 'is Peter Duncan really his real name?' and let me know what it says."

"Yeah…" I said. "It's his real name."

"Weird. Sounds made up. Peter Duncan. Think about it. He's out there dunkin' his peter. See? I always thought Peter Parker was a good porn name. Make a bunch of Spider-Man parodies. He's parking his peter for sure. But instead of web, he's shooting ropes of… you know…"

"So, I need to speak with Mark, I think."

"Let me guess. Brought me back to life so you could bone me, right?"

"Yeah, but now I'm not really into the idea."

"Ugh. Men. Of course you're not. Girl dies in a weird weed and lube accident, shooting porn and all of a sudden, you're too good for her."

"I mean, you just look different…"

"How many times have you said that to Tinder dates?"

"Oh, wow. They're all dogs in real life."

"Yeah?"

"This one girl... she must have been arching her back and pushing her chest forward like a contortionist. Huge jugs, nice ass. But in real life? Sort of flat."

"Did y'all have a good conversation at least?"

"Pssssshhhh, we did, until I found out she looked like that."

"I think I'm getting the picture here."

"Yeah. Check this one out. Look how thin she looks."

"Did you not notice the door frame beside her?"

"What do you mean? Why would I look at a doorframe?"

"Does she live in a funhouse?"

She tapped the image and zoomed in.

The doorframe looked like it was bent like plastic into a half circle. The same curvature as... her hips.

"Holy shit!" I said. "You're already helping me out! Telling this bitch to fuck off."

"Did you ever think the issue is that?"

"The editing? Fuck no. Not until you showed me."

"No, no. The issue is that maybe women, especially in their twenties, are held at such a high beauty standard they feel the need to make their pictures look like they live in a funhouse so they can avoid dudes being shitty to them online?"

"Are you a philosopher or a pornstar? I know why she did it. She's trying to trick alpha males like me into getting her ass pregnant, so we're trapped for life."

"Oh boy, Tanner. We have got a LOT of work to do."

I tossed the implant back and forth in my hand and looked at her deflated tit.

"Yeah," I said. "Looks like we do."

She took the implant from me and stuffed it back into her flesh. It fell out and landed on the floor, making a dull thud. She sighed, picked it up, put it back in, and pointed at the duct tape on my desk.

I handed it to her, and she taped the wound closed.

"Ok," she said. "Now that we've got that issue out of the way." She straightened her back and shook the hair out of her eyes like she was about to say something so important my life would forever change.

"Tanner Henry!" she said. "If I am to be your servant in sexual relations from now until you die, we must restore my former beauty! To do so, I will be giving you tasks to complete. Upon the completion of the last task, I will look as I once looked and be but a servant to your every desire. Sound ok?"

CHAPTER 5
I STILL HAVE NO IDEA WHY I HAD TO DO THAT

I had no idea this dead babe would be so demanding. First, she made me go to a costume store and buy one of those skintight latex body suits, then she had to guide me through trying to make her face look not like a burnt up old hot dog.

Between the bodysuit, the eye patch, the wig, and the makeup that was so thick it looked like a mask; she looked like the world's worst attempt at a sexy pirate costume. It took all night to end up not looking great.

Where the fuck was Marty? He was good at this shit.

"It's not good, but it's done," she said as she stretched her fingers in her gloves. Her implant started to droop a little. She rolled her eyes and shoved it back into place.

"Ok," she said. "Groovy, awesome, amazing. Let's go get some food."

"Do you even need to eat?"

"Probably not. But today is a big day for you. Have you ever bought someone else's lunch?"

"I've bought dinner for chicks before on dates."

"Let me rephrase that. Have you ever bought lunch-"

"Dinner."

"Lunch OR dinner, for someone you didn't want to screw?"

I thought really hard about it.

Nothing came to mind.

I don't even think I've bought dinner for my parents, not lunch either, and definitely not breakfast.

"No. I haven't."

"I had a feeling."

She opened the front door and waved her arm out, hurrying me along.

We drove to Burger King and parked.

"I hope you like BK breakfast," I said.

She looked around the parking lot, then pointed across the street. "Go to Taco Bell."

I drove to Taco Bell and rolled my eyes at her.

When we went inside, she grabbed my arm and let a couple go in front of us. They were in their middle life and kind of looking like they didn't need Taco Bell; but what do I know?

"Tell the cashier you're buying theirs," she said.

"What?" I said. "No fucking way! I don't know these people. Especially not on a breakfast level."

"What's the difference?"

"You buy breakfast for someone who you've... you know... let stay over. If you're getting them breakfast, it was good ass shit. You want to hook up again."

"You're fucking gnarly gross."

"You're a pornstar."

"I suppose that must mean I'm a bad person?"

"It means you sleep with people for less than breakfast."

"Tell my bank account that. And you know what? My former job doesn't reflect who I was as a person - WE'RE GETTING THEIRS! - and the fact that you think it does is a reflection of who you are."

The older couple thanked us and shook my hand.

Why did they shake my hand?

I did not cause this mess.

I guess I did it indirectly through Mark.

"Why did you do that?" I asked.

"You were too busy arguing with me about the moral compass of everything to complete the task I brought you here to accomplish."

"Oh..."

"Yeah. Get a burrito and let's go."

Back in the car, I sipped on my Baja Blast and wondered how far I had set back my goal of getting her hot again. I looked her over; she didn't look bad still. I mean, under all that skintight latex holding it in place was a pretty gross looking corpse, but, hey, I could probably deal with what I was seeing for a handy or BJ.

"I'm not giving you a BJ, HJ, RJ, or any other letter with a J after it until you finish your quest."

I was starting to wonder if she could read my mind or if my gaze was a little heavy.

"And quit staring at me. It's rude."

Mystery solved.

We drove back to my room in awkward silence.

When we got there, Marty and his girlfriend were making out and listening to some bullshit Cryptkeeper music. I paused the music and yelled, "fuck yeah, Marty! Getting sack deep in a big titty goth chick. My man!"

Melinda rolled her eyes, stood up, and left.

"Thanks, Tanner," Marty said. "You're a real fucking winner, you know that?"

I grabbed him by the front of his shirt and shoved him down onto his bed. I got in his face and said, "the fuck you say to me, bitch?"

He got up and stormed out of the door.

I went to follow, but Lena said I couldn't because she knew what my next task was.

CHAPTER 6
NOW I SMELL LIKE BEANS AND BLACK FINGERNAIL POLISH, AND IT SUCKS

Lena made me follow Marty and his big titty goth girlfriend to wherever they were going. They parked in front of a house that had Jack-o'-lanterns proudly painted black with sad faces displayed on the front porch.

It was March.

Not even remotely close to Halloween.

Where did they get the pumpkins?

That was the first thing I checked.

Lena made me get out. She said I had to go apologize to Marty and try to enjoy his company.

When I got to the porch, I touched the Jack-o'-lantern... ceramic.

"Is it real?" Lena asked.

"No," I said. "It's ceramic."

"You knock."

"No, you're making me be here, and I have no clue why. YOU knock."

"Ok. I knock, you talk, deal."

She knocked, and I about shit myself over losing this side of the battle.

The knocker was a fucking gargoyle, by the way.

These people were serious.

The door opened and the music that was sort of faint before poured out in full volume. It was loud, slow, and gloomy. I felt the sound waves wash over me like a wave of depression.

I've never been depressed in my life, but that music made me question what the point of existence on Earth was.

"Oh, hey," I said. "I was curious if Marty was here."

The woman who answered the door was at least six feet tall. She had long black hair, red lipstick, and a giant inverted cross hanging around her neck.

Yeah, she had giant tits, too.

How come Marty got to hang out with all the big titty goth girls and I was stuck with a dead pornstar whose implant won't stay in place?

Speaking of which, she was over there adjusting it at that very second.

"What is your business with Martin?" the woman asked.

"Funny story," I said. "I'm not... entirely sure."

I looked at Lena.

Lena didn't even look up to make eye contact. She just said, "Tanner owes him an apology."

The woman nodded and stepped aside, letting us in.

She guided us through the house into a huge room with black furniture all over. There were paintings of skulls with black frames, black candles everywhere, and the TV was playing concert footage.

Marty, or Martin, whichever, was lying on a couch with his head in Melinda's lap while she brushed his hair.

I could tell he had been crying.

I wanted to beat the fuck out of him right then and there.

"There you are," I said. "I'm fucking sorry, alright? Cool. See you all later."

I turned to leave, and Lena was staring at me with her one eye like she was going to disembowel me.

Marty stood up and walked over to me. He had tears in his eyes, and he said, "I don't know what to do, Tanner. I try ridiculously hard to have a good relationship with you. I know we're from different worlds. But couldn't you try?"

"Marty," I said. "Or Martin, I don't even know what you go by. You piss me off. You're such a massive shit stain. You're all sad and gloomy about everything, and it just makes me want to beat the fuck out of you all the time."

"Imagine how we feel about you," Melinda said as she stood up and got in my face.

"See," I said. "You need your big titty goth girlfriend to rescue you. It's shameful."

While that wonderful statement was in the air, it turned into a little birdie and landed on a shoulder. A massive man wearing fishnet sleeves and black eyeliner stood up and looked at me with the fury of a million exploding kittens. He walked over to me and put his extremely muscular chest in my face.

He towered over me.

He could have had one hell of a career in the NBA if he apparently wasn't so sad.

"You know," I said. "At least this guy has his failed basketball career to be sad about. But you two-"

I couldn't finish.

I was flying.

I was now the birdie.

Literally being carried like it was nothing.

I landed chest first on a table with food on it. When I rolled off, I noticed I was covered in smashed hot dogs and baked beans.

The giant was towering over me. He was pulling his massive fist back to end my existence like I was the last spark of joy left floating in the dark recesses of his soul.

The woman who opened the door grabbed his arm and said, "Armand, we've talked about this."

He lowered his arm and looked at the ground in shame.

"I could let him hurt you," she said, kneeling by me. "But that's exactly what you keep doing to our sweet Martin. Armand is Melinda's big brother. He spent six years in the marines, and now he's a competitive weightlifter. He also teaches Muy Thai for a living."

"I'm a goner," I said.

"No, he's just mad that you keep doing mean things to Melinda and Martin. My name is Eloise." She extended her hand; I took it, and she helped me up.

Armand, if that was even his real name, I'm guessing not, brushed me off and looked at the baked beans on his hand. "Still got some glizzy on you," he said, brushing off mushed bits of hot dog.

"My friend Tanner is an intolerable asshole," said Lena. "I'm sorry about that. It's my duty to make him learn how to not be completely fucking intolerable."

"I like your body suit," said Eloise.

"Thanks, it has pockets."

"Does it really?"

"No. I couldn't be so lucky. Anyway, can we hang out with you all for a bit? I think if Tanner got to know you all a little better, maybe he wouldn't be such an insensitive asshole to people who like different things than him."

Everyone looked at Marty, who just nodded his head. Fucking wild. I had done nothing but make his life miserable, and here he was trying to help me in some way.

Anyway, we partied pretty hard.

They broke out all of this booze, turned on some band called Christian Death, and we all just had a great time.

There was a point when I was having a drunken heart to heart with Marty about how I shouldn't be mean to him. I explained that I think it comes from a place of jealousy because I see how happy he is and how happy Melinda is to have him around. The only joy I had with another person like that came in twenty-minute bursts before an orgasm.

I realized I hadn't even looked at Melinda or Eloise's chest the whole time I was talking to Marty.

I made eye contact with Lena, and she had this little smile like I had finally done something right. She came over and sat beside me. She turned herself so that she was leaning her back against the armrest of the sofa and her legs were stretched out across me.

I could feel how tight her leg muscles were; I could also feel how tight my pants were becoming in a certain area since part of her left ass cheek was on top of my thigh.

It was still firm.

I took a swig of this nasty ass black sludge beer they gave me and let the moment live as its own.

The next morning, I woke up with dried baked beans and squashed hot dogs on my chest, and my fingernails painted black.

Eloise was already awake and making coffee. She had on a black nightgown and her cleavage was out for the world to see.

I questioned why I spent so much time not staring at it the night before and let my eyes drown in the glorious sight.

"He's a work in progress," Lena said, grabbing my ear and twisting so hard I thought it would rip off. "Thanks for everything!"

CHAPTER 7
WENDY AND HER GODDAMNED MANTIS ARMY AND WHY YOU SHOULD NOT FUCK AROUND WITH THEM

Do you know how hard it is to remove the smell of baked beans and glizzy from your chest hair? The shit had been soaking in the whole night like some weird sort of odor hair dye.

Armand, you bitch.

Don't tell him I said that. I think we're cool now, but I like my arms unbroken.

Lena asked if she could use my phone while I took a nap. I told her as long as she didn't get me into anymore goth parties or buying people Taco Bell, that's cool.

She wanted to check on her husband and make sure he was ok.

"You're married?" I asked.

"Was," she said.

"How did THAT work? Was he in porn?"

"No. Not at all. It worked great."

"He was cool watching you go get railed by like twelve dudes in one day? Sometimes at the same time?"

"Our relationship wasn't based around sex. We loved each other. We enjoyed the same movies, we loved hiking, we used to go kayaking every weekend."

"Fucking guy had the sex life of a god, I bet. How many chicks did he bang with you? Lucky prick."

"Ugh. You have to understand something. All sex isn't porn sex. We made love, lots of kissing, close contact. When I made porn, that was just fucking."

"There's a difference?"

"And this is why you remain single and ready to mingle."

"I'm not getting tied to anyone."

"Listen, Tanner. Getting bent over and plowed away at is fun, it has its place. But there is also sex that calls for intimacy with your partner, the sex where you both want to be as close to each other as you possibly can. Not every woman wants you to go as hard as you can, as fast as you can, and erupt in two minutes every single time. Porn was porn. But we had something different."

Her eyes glowed a little when she talked about him.

I gotta be honest here. That was the first moment I started feeling like I could give someone that glow in their eyes.

I didn't feel like dealing with that then, though.

"Right... yeah... you can use my phone. Just don't

accidentally like any of his pictures or send a pissed off message when you see he's shagging some other chick a week after you're dead. Goodnight."

I woke up to a weird girl in my room wearing a bright sundress and holding an aquarium.

I sat up and said, "ok, what the fuck?"

She turned around and stared at me with these insane eyes. She had a Praying Mantis on each of her shoulders.

Lena did that cough people do when they want your attention, so I turned to see if she had an explanation for this insanity.

"Her name is Wendy," she said. "She came knocking with all of these Praying Mantises, saying something about how you tricked her, and she would not tolerate evil men."

"We bite the heads off evil men at dawn!" Wendy yelled.

"Jesus Christ, Wendy," I said. "I told you I was sorry, and this wasn't going to work out."

"You sent me a friend request, a message that said 'hey,' then you sent me a picture of your... weird... kinda crooked-"

"Ok! Stop! I'm sorry! I told you I was drunk."

"Hold on," said Lena. "You said one word and THEN sent a dick pic?"

"That's what I always do."

"Does it ever work?"

"Not really. Usually just ends with me calling them a bitch."

"You did call me a bitch after I said, 'a lil crooked, ain't it?'"

"Of course, I did, you-"

I jumped up and instantly fell back.

What I'm about to say will sound like a lie, but I swear to God one of the fucking things pulled its little arms back like it was about to fuck me up worse than a football bat.

"That's Brian," Wendy said. "She watches too many horror movies and gets a little stab happy. Total gorehound."

"Can you please leave?"

"Sorry, this other one," she shrugged her shoulder up and down. If the other mantis was a person, it would have been a balding British man with a mustache that was judging me. "That's Adam, she's hella political. She wants to make sure I right the injustice you've caused."

"Is she Batman? Why did you bring two praying mantises here?"

"Seven actually. And that's because they're my army of Praying Mantises and we've come to murder you for calling me a bitch."

"Seems like a little bit of a harsh punishment for the crime."

"The crime was the picture of your tallywhacker. The punishment was Caitlin and Yolanda's idea. Elford said we should leave you in the woods for a cryptid. Sarah Jane was cool with that because she loves the woods and just wants to wrap this up and get to cake. Denise actually wanted to grow a giant Venus flytrap and let it eat you."

"I'm losing track of all these names. I really am."

"That's why I left Eady at home. I thought eight was a bit overkill."

All the mantises ran up her arms. She was Willard of mantis. The tiger king of... are praying mantises' insects?

I gasped and leaned back. "Willard! No!" I yelled. "I'll get you your raise! I won't foreclose on your mother's house! I won't fire you! Please don't let them sting me!"

"Actually," Wendy said. "They don't sting. Common misconception is that all little creatures sting. Did you know that ancient people may have thought they were fairies? Pretty cool, huh? Also, I have no idea what you're talking about."

"I think you've proven your point, Wendy," Lena said, stepping in. "He's pissed all over himself."

"Serves him right."

With that, all the fairies or death machines went back in the aquarium and left with Wendy. The door opened an instant after she closed it and she said, "Eady! I told you to stay at home! Come on!"

Another mantis flew out the door.

We heard her telling Caitlin it was a good idea and thanking Yolanda for slightly tweaking it to scaring the piss out of me, as opposed to killing me.

"Lena," I said. "What the fuck just happened?"

"You pissed your pants. Before that, she knocked, I answered, she asked if she could come in. I thought the mantises were cool as hell. Did you see how she has them trained?"

"That was a total violation of my privacy and a disregard to my safety."

"So was sending an unwarranted dick pic. I bet that... thing... which I heard was crooked by the way... scared her worse than those mantises scared you."

I shook my head. Fuck this. This was insanity.

"She was at dinner with her dad. The image preview popped up. Do you know how uncomfortable that was? Just because a woman is friendly, that doesn't mean she wants to see your dick, friend."

I started thinking about that.

Yeah, that was probably really awkward.

Yeah, I probably shouldn't be allowed to have my phone when I'm blitzed at five pm.

"It was a shitty thing to do, and you deserved worse," Lena said, just really trying to drive the point home.

I have to admit, I turned and saw the pain in her eye.

"Has this happened to you?" I asked.

"All the time," she said. "Men think because I make porn and have a spicy site that I must be some sex obsessed nymphomaniac. I'm a human being, Tanner. These things I do don't give anyone else the right to violate my personal space and boundaries. Me doing what I do isn't consent for every weird asshole to show me their cock on the internet."

"Why don't you just shrug it off and move on? What do you expect?"

"To be treated like a human being. When I make videos and content, when I post pictures; I'm consenting for you all to see that moment. I'm not consenting to people approaching me twenty-four seven like it's all I do. It's disrespectful, it's hurtful, and it's demoralizing. Men seem to think that because they've seen me naked that they own me. That's the same thing you did to that weird bug girl. You didn't even see her naked. Are those even bugs?"

"I need to Google it, actually. It would be a nice change of pace from all this preachiness."

"You made her feel smaller than small. You made her feel like all she was to the world was a piece of flesh to be served up to a horny customer rush at the hot dog stand. Get your shit together."

Goddamn.

That one opened a wound.

She was right. I had to stop and think about it.

When there's a dead person telling you this shit, you know it's true. What do they have to lose?

I went on Facebook and sent Wendy a message apologizing. She sent back the middle finger emoji and a picture of her mantises.

I deserved that I guess.

"Lena," I said. "Please don't let anymore weird bug girls try to kill me while I sleep. You want to go to the library and see if we can find out if mantises are bugs? They have a huge wildlife section. That's where I did all my dugong research."

"What in the Hell is a Dugong?"

"Holy shit..."

I explained on the way to the library.

CHAPTER 8
I WATCHED LENA AND THE ANNOYING LIBRARIAN BOND OVER A CONVERSATION ABOUT TWITTER THAT I DIDN'T UNDERSTAND BECAUSE I REALLY JUST USE IT TO SEND CHICKS PICTURES OF MY DONG.

"... so, you see, the pollution is ruining the Dugong's grass habitat. That's why they are becoming endangered," I was wrapping up my soapbox about the Dugong. Cute little fuckers. Why does no one seem to care about them? I mean, sure, Manatees are more popular; but that doesn't take away from the fact that some horrible environmental injustices are being committed against the Dugong.

It isn't fair.

Lena made her way to the librarian, which, by the way, does she ever go home?

She just straight up asked her, "are Praying Mantises insects?"

The girl slowly moved her head from side to side with those annoying Pixar eyes and said, "you know, that's a good question. Let me ask Twitter."

"Oh gross. Twitter is the WORST!"

"I know, but sometimes I get some funny responses. I have eleven K followers because one time I was filming my friend trying to break into her house, and when she hit the door really hard she actually shit all over herself. Went viral. Now people think I'm funny. Who knew! I didn't even have to crap my pants!"

"Twitter. The place where we can have deep thoughtful conversations with experts in any field on any subject. We can connect with our role models and favorite people. We can meet someone across the planet who likes the same cartoon from the nineties as us and build a really meaningful friendship. Instead, we usually use it to watch people shit themselves. Both metaphorically and literally."

"The duality of man."

"Hey," I said. "It's me, Tanner, why are we here exactly? We need a book about mantises. Not a convo about Twitter."

"I don't know why you're here," the annoying librarian said, "but since you haven't asked, my name is Elsa. Yeah, like Frozen. It sucks. I know you're Tanner.

This is Lena White, who you brought back from the dead. The books are over there but, OH! We got an answer... 'get fucking real bitch. Everyone knows Praying Mantises are part of an order of insect that has twenty-four hundred species in about four hundred and sixty genera in thirty-three families. Now post a topless pic.'"

"What did you say?" I asked.

"I said, 'get fucking real, bitch-"

"Not that!"

"Oh, I told him I wasn't doing that unless he at least took me to Arby's first. It's already at ten likes."

"Jesus Christ, why is talking to either of you so fucking hard?"

"You know," said Lena. "That's a lot of words. Did that exceed the character limit?"

"Good question!" Elsa said before typing on her phone. "Yeah, it totally fits."

"Maybe it just seems wordy. Anyway, now we know. What time do you get off tonight, Elsa?"

"In like two hours. Why? What's up?"

"I was going to make Tanner here invite you to dinner."

"I'm not doing that," I said.

"Why? She's nice enough."

Elsa rolled her eyes and said, "he doesn't think I'm attractive enough. He's very superficial. Have you not noticed?"

"I have to admit, when I met him, I had a hunch he didn't bring me back from the grave for my bubbly personality."

"Isn't it the most cringe thing?"

"He's absolutely insufferable."

"Hey," I said. "I'm right here!"

"Still," Lena said. "I can see some good in him. It's in his eyes. If you look in his eyes, you can see this whole act is some sort of coverup for some weird toxic masculinity he learned growing up."

"I hate when that happens. Toxic masculinity and someone just tells you the internal plot of your personal movie like that. Very cliché. He is cute, though. Like a little puppy that tries to be scary but is honestly just a cuddle bug."

"Too true! Tanner, invite this woman to dinner! It's part of your quest!"

I closed my eyes and said, "Elsa, would you like to go to dinner together?"

"Groovy!" she said. "I know the perfect place! What kind of a quest are you on?"

"Oh, that," said Lena. "He's on a... 'quest' ...to restore me to my former beauty."

"Ohhhhh, a 'quest,' gotcha."

They may as well have winked at each other.

Air quotes and all.

I was sorta pissed. Was this all some sort of cosmic

prank?

What the fuck was the 'in' joke here?

Was I not going to get sack deep?

Goddamnit.

"Sure," said Elsa. "I would actually love to go to dinner with you."

She smiled and shrugged. Her cheeks were turning red, and she had a faint hint of that glow I liked in Lena's one crusty ass eye.

When she went to get a piece of paper to write her number down, I looked at her ass.

It really was a pretty great ass.

Maybe I was going through a phase?

I mean, Lena is what I would call thick too, but in, like, a pornstar way, you know?

Elsa was five foot nothing with wide hips and medium-sized tits.

Not to mention the red hair wasn't exactly my thing either.

I have been accused of being shallow before, but really, I just have a type and Elsa wasn't it.

When she turned around, she looked at my phone. Her mouth turned into this sideways little smile. It was awkward, dorky, and cute AF. She picked up my phone and added herself to my contacts as "Elsa rulz."

She did a little giggle at that.

She made eye contact with me, and her mouth slowly opened like she was embarrassed.

"Thanks... pal," I said, starting to feel really uncomfortable myself.

On the way out of the library, Lena hit her hips against mine and said, "I saw you checking out her booty."

I looked at her like I was mad as hell and about to strike her.

"You can act mad if you want," she said, "but I saw it. I can't blame you. She has a great ass. She's a cutie and I think you two would be cute together if she could remove your head from your ass."

I didn't say anything.

I was a little pissed off because maybe Lena was right?

Maybe I was just having a weird moment where I wanted her to be right because of that eye glow they were both good at?

The duality of man.

CHAPTER 9
YOU MEET SOME WILD PEOPLE IF YOU DECIDE TO GO OUTSIDE

The first issue I had with the place Elsa took us was that I got a fork with a bent arm. Are they called arms? Spokes? I don't know. I thought about asking Elsa, but she would have asked Twitter and I didn't need that whole conversation again.

After the mantises I was about sick of hearing about dick pics.

"My fork is bent," I said, holding it up to Elsa.

"Is that called an... arm?" Lena asked.

"Oh!" said Elsa. "Good question! I'll ask Twitter."

Goddamnit.

"I wouldn't ask Twitter what anything long and pointy is called," said Lena.

"Good call," said Elsa.

"Can we PLEASE just have dinner without talking

about dick pics?" I asked. "I'm so sick of hearing about dick pics."

"If you're sick of hearing about them," said Lena. "Imagine how sick we are of receiving them."

"Walked right into that one, didn't ya?" asked Elsa.

Elsa and Lena high fived after that.

The man in the booth behind us ducked and turned around like his life was in danger.

"Hey!" he said. "Watch out now! I was in a serious fireworks accident. I'm really sensitive to hearing loud noises like that in public. I could almost feel my finger getting blown up again."

"I'm so sorry," Elsa said. "One of my friends from high school was missing a couple fingers because a fire-cracker blew up in his hand."

"Mine was one of them little popper things. Burned the shit out of my skin. Miserable experience. Especially scary because I need my hands for a living."

"Wait," said Lena. "You can't hear me give my friend... we're friends, right?"

"Absolutely, we're friends!" said Elsa.

"You can't hear me give my friend a high five without thinking about a small little burn on your finger from a small firework? Are those even fireworks?"

"Actually," he said. "It was from a Jalapeño popper. Too hot out of the fryer. The sound just reminds me of those things. Then I think about popper and remember the burn."

"What the fuck is he on about?" Elsa asked. She looked at me and threw her arms up when she asked.

"Harold!" said the server, walking over. "You cannot be serious. You will find anyway to talk about that damn Jalapeño popper in here. Harold here has been trying to get a free lunch for fifteen years telling that story. My name is Kyra. I'm your server today. What'll ya have to drink?"

"I'll have coffee," said Elsa.

The server walked away.

I guess the rest of us don't count for shit.

She came back with three coffees.

When she sat them down, she looked to Elsa and said, "usual?"

Elsa nodded, and she left again.

"Is she just ignoring our existence?" I asked.

"Probably," said Lena as she sipped on her coffee.

I sat there staring out the window for ten minutes, just absolutely stewing.

I wanted to order a cheeseburger and fries.

That was what I wanted.

I wanted it with tomato, bacon, lettuce.

No mayonnaise.

A BLT with a burger and cheese.

I got lucky because that's what was on the plate that sat down in front of me.

I looked up at Elsa and started to ask if she brought us to a mind reader diner.

A psychic cafe.

A... I'm out of them.

I noticed Lena and Elsa had the same thing.

"She just gave us all my usual order," Elsa said. "I like the BLT on grilled sourdough, but as a burger."

The grilled sourdough was a nice touch.

I made a mental note to remember that one.

"So," Elsa said, taking a bite out of her burger. "What other things do you have to do on this quest?"

Lena put a finger over my mouth to shoosh me and started talking.

"Well," she said. "We're three or four tasks in. He's doing better than he did at the first one. But he still needs some work. I don't really have a set plan for what these tasks should be. I'm open to ideas, is what I'm trying to say."

"Hmmmmm," Elsa said. "Let me think about it a bit."

They both grinned at each other.

Yeah, I was definitely on the outside of an inside joke.

"What was it like being in porn?" Elsa just straight up asked. No hesitation. Just flat out addressed it like she was working at McDonalds.

"It was a good living," said Elsa. "I only had to film

once a week. Sometimes not even that. And with Only Fans being so popular now, sometimes all I had to do was film by myself at home."

"Oh, ok, nice."

"Nice?" I said, looking at them both. "Ask her about... her HUSBAND!"

"You were married?" asked Elsa.

Lena rolled her eyes and said, "Tanner can't get past that."

"Your husband was a cuck," I said.

"A duck?" Elsa asked.

"A cuck!"

"Like a quack quack?"

"No! A cuck. Like a man who watches his spouse get boned by other... are you having a fucking laugh?"

She was.

Elsa was covering her mouth and giggling.

She was playing me like a flute.

Here I was, trying to get Lena to play a certain part of my body like a flute, and I was being played like one in a metaphorical sense.

"My husband," Lena said. "Supported my career. Of course, how could he not? He was able to work part-time because of it. And besides, we had an understanding. He knew the difference."

"Did he ever watch you make movies?" asked Elsa.

I blew air out of my nose and shook my head. Why would she ask that?

"He did," said Lena. "He was curious about what happened on set one time, so he came and watched. It was a group scene. In between takes, he would bring me water and wipe the sweat out of my eyes."

"That's so sweet," said Elsa.

"Sounds pretty gross to me!" said the finger burn man.

"Hey," I said. "Why don't you mind your own business and let us enjoy our lunch?"

"You sat there. I was already here."

"Nope. You sat down after us."

"Didn't either."

"Did."

"Didn't either."

"Did."

"Didn't either."

"Did. Did. Did. Did. Did. Did! And you fucking know it!"

"Yeah... ok... I guess I did. You have to understand. I don't get out much. My wife passed away around five years ago. The only conversation I usually get through the day is harassing the wait staff here about the time that popper burnt my finger."

"Sorry, bro. I didn't have any idea. The whole finger thing must have been traumatic."

An awkward silence fell over the diner, and he said, "Just wish I had someone to come over and watch my videos with me. That's all I need. Just someone to do that. Then maybe I wouldn't be so lonely and miserable. Anyway, guess I'll just die alone with my burnt-up finger."

"Oh," said Elsa. "I know your next task."

I rolled my eyes, turned to the guy, and said, "hey, we'll come watch your videos. What time?"

He was overjoyed and stood up.

He clenched his fists and looked at me, then he said, "six o'clock! Here's my address!"

He handed me a business card and left.

Harold McGurvey–Growing Up Socks.

There was another name scratched out with a pen...

I showed it to Lena and Elsa and said, "what the fuck?"

"It's his business," Kyra said, popping up like she could teleport. "He used to run it with his sister. They were pretty popular. But then they got in some argument and split up."

She set the bill down and left.

"Great," I said. "Now you've got me watching sock puppet videos with a stranger."

"Actually," Elsa said. "I was going to suggest you help him set up a YouTube account so he could just post his videos there. We don't know this guy; we could end up dead! No offense Lena."

I closed my eyes and took a deep breath.

I was going to snap.

I could feel it.

"None taken," said Lena as she chomped down on her burger and pushed her implant back up into place. "This thing has really been slipping. May need to go put some more tape on it."

CHAPTER 10
SOCK PUPPETS AND RECONCILIATION

Harold's house was alright.

It was just a little two-story job.

I could tell he was reluctant about us going to the second floor because he kept saying, "don't go up to the second floor, please."

Not one of us were trying to so I don't get the anxiety with that one.

It was fucking creepy, though.

It had started raining when we got there. So, it was your classic dark and stormy night in a stranger's house cliché. It seemed like every time he warned us about upstairs, lightning struck.

He was showing us all of these weird ass home movies he made with his sister.

They were all sock puppet shows and, quite frankly pretty fucking weird.

I think we were all starting to get a really creepy vibe from the guy.

It's a dude, who is like sixty, mind you, and a woman who would have had to be in her fifties, doing a sock puppet show about hygiene and shit for a bunch of kindergartners.

I always wondered about shit like this.

Remember Steve from Blue's Clues?

What did he do in his off time?

Did he just act that wholesome everywhere he went, or did he turn into a different guy?

Imagine you're Steve and you're out buying an R-rated movie and a 4Loko for a nice Friday evening. Imagine then that you hear a little kid say they recognize you; how do you explain that? How do you explain the fact that you got all this shit because you've got a girl you met two nights ago coming over? How do you explain to the kid where Blue is? Do you just let mommy do all the work while at the same time trying to get her number, because while you're not trying to be a stepdad, mommy got some real milf vibes going on?

What do you do?

I wouldn't be thinking about this at all, but a couple weeks back a girl I went to high school with posted a show her kids were watching. The host was a woman in her twenties and the shirt she was wearing mixed with the camera angle made it really obvious her nipples were pierced.

Weird, right?

It's like we think these people are the characters they play even off screen. Of course, this girl had her nipples pierced. Of course, Steve tries to fuck her while the Texas Chainsaw Massacre remake plays in the background.

Humans are fucking complex.

The puppets on the screen were talking about how important friendship and shit is.

I about puked.

A whole lot of caring and sharing shit.

"You know," Elsa said. "Have you tried calling your sister?"

"No," said Harold. "She'll call me first. This is her fault."

I shrugged because I could not have possibly given a fuck less.

I was sort of convinced he killed his sister.

Elsa made eye contact with me, and I could tell she thought the same.

But then Lena was staring at me like I had to do something; so, I asked if I could use the bathroom.

He said sure, but don't go upstairs.

Naturally, I went upstairs, right?

Wasn't that what Lena was trying to tell me to do?

Then we could call the cops, dude would get arrested for murder, and we'd be happy as can be.

There were three rooms; one was a bedroom, the other a bathroom, and the third had a closed door.

I assumed this was where the secrets were hidden so I opened it.

I now know where your socks go when they come up missing. In this room, there had to be at least a thousand sock puppets. There was a little booth in the corner that looked like the stage. I walked in and looked around. No wonder he didn't want us coming up here.

A flash of lightning struck, and I swear some of them moved toward me. I promise you I am not making this up. I heard little feet run across the floor, and the sound of the puppets whispering. He didn't kill his sister; the puppets did.

I turned to run and hit face first into a low hanging beam. I fell onto a table and rolled down onto the floor. A computer screen turned on atop a desk above me. It was open to Harold's email account. I snooped through it a little to see what he did to make these sock puppets come to life. I was really hoping he had used Mark because I needed to get in touch with the guy. All I found were a bunch of sad emails he wrote about trying to talk things out with someone, but they were all in his drafts. I found a stack of business cards sitting on a shelf; it had Harold's number and a woman named Priscilla.

I think I found the sister.

When I went to the bathroom, I decided I should try to squeeze out a log or two while I had the chance. But while doing that, I could go ahead and text Harold's sister.

I explained that I was a friend and Harold was all tore up; she said he needed to reach out first; I explained that the third party reach out absolves either party of having to reach out first and she should just go ahead and come over.

Twenty minutes later, I was washing my hands and listening to Harold and Priscilla scream at each other.

When I walked into the room, Harold charged me. His body was moving so fast it whipped his head back. He tackled me into a wall and started yelling about me going into the workshop.

I thought I was dead.

Lena twisted his ear and pulled him off me.

Elsa said, "alright, can we try to talk this out?"

Priscilla stormed off upstairs.

"Damn you," said Harold. "She can only talk about her feelings in character."

Five minutes later, Lena, Elsa, and I were watching two sock puppets argue with each other about some problem we didn't have enough context for.

The woman puppet bit the man puppet in his sock neck. The man screamed in agony. Red confetti flew up from below the booth and landed all over the room.

"This is pretty fucking weird," said Lena.

Elsa shook her head, walked over to the booth, and grabbed both puppets by their necks.

She lifted them up until the human faces of the puppeteers were showing.

"Listen," Elsa said. "Either y'all figure this out like adults, or we're outta here."

"I'm confused about who you people even are," said Priscilla.

"I met them at the diner," said Harold. "They said they had some interest in sock puppet shows."

"No one does anymore, Harold. That's what I tried to explain. The kids are growing up and want something more modern. That's why I said we needed special effects."

"Sock puppets with special effects… get real!"

"I've been making YouTube videos and they've been a hit! I just wish… I don't know… never mind."

"What?"

"I just wish my big brother would stop being so stubborn because I want to try something new, and he'd join me for a little while."

Harold got all misty eyed and hugged Priscilla. He promised he would come along and help, but he still wanted to do the live shows here and there.

"Hold the fuck up," I said. "Y'all stopped talking because she wanted to make puppets breathe fire or something?"

"No," said Harold. "I thought she wanted to go her own way without me."

With that, they both started crying. They hugged each other and made promises about sock puppet shows.

I left.

I just marched out the front door and left.

Lena and Elsa must have followed me because Lena sat down saying, "gotta be honest. I thought he didn't want us to go upstairs because he was a serial killer."

I spun around and faced her in the back seat and said, "YOU!" with as scary a face as I could make.

Lena and Elsa laughed.

"I thought I was about to be on a meat hook," said Elsa. "The way he kept making us watch puppet movies was unsettling."

I dug my palms into the steering wheel and felt so annoyed.

What the fuck just happened?

Why did I just accidentally play Dr. Phil?

Did I just reunite the single most fucking obnoxious act in the world?

"Hey," said Lena as she rubbed my shoulder. "You did something good there."

"Honestly," said Elsa. "You really did. When you were

taking so long, I thought you were either dead or taking a giant shit. I kept wondering if we were in some sort of Psycho situation and his sister was actually dead and he was going to slap on a wig and kill us. Grief makes people do funny things."

"The duality of man."

"Really, you did good there, Tanner. I knew there was something good deep down inside when you wrote about the Dugongs."

I looked in the rear-view mirror at Elsa. She had that look in her eyes, that glow. Only this time, it was a little brighter. Maybe she did see something in me, maybe she just really liked being in weird situations like this. I don't know, but that look shot right into my heart. I looked at Lena; she was smirking at me. She did a little slow nod, like I was a good little doggy doing the right thing.

I had enough.

No one fucks around with my emotions.

CHAPTER 11
I PLANNED FOR VENGEANCE TO BE MINE, BUT I JUST SORTA BORROWED IT

I couldn't nail down a plan on how exactly to show them I was furious.

I was honestly a little hurt.

I felt like I was being tricked.

I mean, I KNEW I was being tricked.

I had this whole plan in my head; we'd go back to the library and find another book about spells or shit. Something I'd pretend I found to bring Lena back to life for real.

She'd be all stoked to see her cuck husband, then I'd make her do stupid shit. Then I'd drop it on her that I was lying.

Having a laugh.

Just a little Josh is all that is.

Little life lesson, so to speak.

I suggested going to the library; I got that far.

When we were inside, I started to feel really bad. I didn't think Lena was doing anything malicious to me. Was I annoyed that I had been tricked? Yes. It hurt my ego pretty badly.

What was I doing?

I couldn't do that to her.

That glow she got in her eyes was the same one I probably got talking about Dugong.

The same one Elsa was starting to get for me.

I was becoming Elsa's Dugong.

You can't take away someone's dugong.

ESPECIALLY not Lena's, she was the reason I was someone else's Dugong.

I felt like Lena genuinely cared about making me into a better person. I didn't know how any of the things she was forcing me to do would make me a better person, but I thought she was trying.

Truth is, she was sort of my friend at that point. I started to feel a sentimental attachment to her, other than trying to get her back to what she used to look like so I could get laid.

I had been thinking more about Elsa in that way than Lena. I had been thinking of Elsa in other ways more. I genuinely enjoying spending time with her. She seemed to think there was something fun to be around about me.

I hate to admit it, but maybe I was developing a little crush?

It didn't matter.

I couldn't go through with my original plan.

Instead, I said I wanted some books on Dugong.

I was giving a nice speech about how important conservation is to the Dugong habitat when I noticed Elsa seemed uncharacteristically distracted. They were both sitting criss-cross-applesauce on the floor in an aisle way, giving me their full attention. But something started to feel off about Elsa.

I started talking about something else; I think it was making pepperoni pizza on a strawberry Pop-Tart. Lena noticed immediately and gagged. I asked Elsa what she thought, and she said, "you are so right. The Dugong is such a special creature. We have to do whatever we can to protect it at all costs."

I squinted my eyes at her, and she knew she was had.

"You haven't been talking about that, have you?" she asked. "I'm sorry. I got an upsetting message."

"Can I see?" asked Lena. "Oh, GROSS!"

They wouldn't let me see.

I kept asking and begging.

Elsa was crying a little and Lena hugged her close.

What the fuck?

Did someone die?

"What is that?!" I yelled, pointing behind them. When they turned around, I snatched Elsa's phone from her lap.

A dick pic.

There was a dick pic.

I shook my head.

"Scroll up," Elsa said.

As if the dick pic wasn't bad enough, there were messages from this guy talking to Elsa about things she was really into. She sent him messages about books she read, pottery class with her mom, all of this really sweet stuff you only share with someone you want to either be friends with or have a relationship with.

I had done this type of thing before.

This guy didn't even read any of her messages. I could tell by the one and two word responses to Elsa's novella sizone- or two-words just playing along and waiting for his moment to strike.

I felt my brain go hot.

That's how mad I was.

I was defying scientific logic.

"I thought," Elsa said as she sniffed. "I thought he genuinely wanted to be my friend."

The message before the dick pic was Elsa talking about checking out the damn sock puppet show. He took the chance and sent, "I got something you can put a sock on..."

That's not even a good play.

Mans has zero rizz.

Mr. No-Rizz.

He was probably drunk.

I could tell by the sudden boldness and lack of patience to get what he wanted.

"I'm sorry," I said.

Lena and Elsa looked at me like I just recited the constitution.

"I'm so fucking sorry," I said again as I began to feel my eyes getting too heavy.

I sat on the ground beside Elsa and pulled her to me. She melted into my arms and let me hold her while she sobbed.

She didn't know how much she was comforting me, too.

I really fucked up.

I fucked up over and over and over again.

Lena was typing a message back to the guy on Elsa's phone when it hit me.

"I have an idea," I said.

CHAPTER 12
VENGEANCE WAS MINE ANYWAY, JUST IN A DIFFERENT WAY, LIKE A BATMAN WAY

"Hello? Elsa?"

That was the fucking dickhead.

His name was Randy, and he was a fucking turd ready to be flushed down the toilet of life.

I know he's an idiot because he agreed to meet Elsa in a library after closing.

He really believed sending that pic with his lame ass pick up line was all he had to do.

I don't even think I was that dumb.

Maybe I was.

I think about if I would have stumbled into a dark creepy library looking for sex, and I realize, yeah, I absolutely would have done that.

My crooked dick would have guided me like the arrow of a compass, and I would have done the exact same thing as this fucking idiot.

I would have come walking into this library with pizza and beer.

I would have had a whole plan about setting up some books as a little platform.

I probably would have tried to set that up and got annoyed and impatient and just tried to have sex on the counter.

No fucks given about a camera or anything.

Two minutes of pleasure outweigh everything else.

That's exactly where Randy was.

He was thinking about how fucking cool he had to be that this worked.

Lena was hiding in one of the aisles, waiting. "Hey," she said. "Elsa left for the night, but I asked her to have you come, in more ways than one. Looks like I'm going to have to do the second half."

Randy looked down the aisle Lena was in and watched in amazement.

Lena had set up a cell phone flashlight as a backlight. Her silhouette was bold against the light. She danced slowly and ran her hands across her body.

I could feel myself getting worked up, so I knew Randy had to be going through it.

She bent over and moved her ass up and down, giving Randy a full view of everything she had to offer. She turned around and unzipped the front of her body suit just enough that her cleavage was hanging out. By the limited light, you couldn't see anything wrong with any of her.

She gave Randy a come-hither motion with her finger, and he practically ran to her.

Elsa and I were on the second-floor walkway behind Randy, watching it all happen. We made sure we had the best view in the place.

Randy got to Lena and leaned in for a kiss. He was so awkward about it; he had his tongue out the whole way. Lena put her finger up to his mouth and said, "don't you want to see... everything?" She ran her hands down her body and did a little twisty dance motion.

"Uh," Randy said. "Yeah, baby, yeah."

Lena undid her body suit all the way. She turned away from him and stepped out of it.

When she turned around, I flipped the light switch.

Randy screamed and fell to the ground.

Lena's body had gotten worse. She looked like some of the wounds had completely dried up and crusted over. She ran at Randy with her arms out, he crawled backwards screaming.

Her implant fell out, and she bent over to pick it up. She held it out to Randy like a demon offering Satan the heart of a Christian.

"Here, Randy," she said. "Isn't this what you wanted? To touch my tits! To feel my body! Now you're going to get your wish, you're going to fuck me for... ETERNITY!"

She let out the most amazing evil laugh I had ever heard. I wish I had recorded it. She could have played a villain in any movie with that laugh. It was loud, awful, and penetrated every part of my senses in the worst way.

She leaped on Randy and pinned him down.

She grabbed his hands and forced him to touch her chest.

He was crying now.

"Randy," she moaned. "Oh, RANDY! Yes! Yes! YEEEESSSS!!!!!"

All of a sudden, I remembered why I wanted to bring her back to life.

I said, "wow..." and Elsa elbowed me in my stomach. I coughed and shrugged.

Whoops a daisy.

Lena leaned her chest in close to his face and ran her hands up across her one remaining tit. She wrapped her arms around her neck and pulled the wig off, exposing her burnt to a sizzle head.

Randy screamed again, and Lena matched it in volume.

She sounded like she was finishing up.

She leaned forward and embraced Randy like she had just finished the greatest orgasm she had ever had.

"Thank you, Randy," she said as she stood up from his body. "I want you to know, every time you send an unasked-for dick pic, it will be me that you'll meet. It will be me for ETERNITY!"

That laugh again.

Goddamn, that laugh.

Randy leaped to his feet and ran out the front door, screaming.

Lena gave us two thumbs up and an awkward little dance.

"Beat that, Wendy!" she yelled and then looked around for fear of the mantises overhearing her.

CHAPTER 13
THE STUPID BOWL OF STUPID SOUP THAT STUPID LIFE GIVES YOU ON A STUPID AFTERNOON

Finally.

It was going to happen.

I had done so much shit to get to this point; not too much, but the sock puppets make up for a lot of fucking annoyance in my book. I also got my ass kicked by a goth guy named after a vampire. I'd say we're even.

I felt like I had won an award.

I didn't even prepare a speech or anything.

I breathed in deep and said, "so, let's do this."

Lena said, "looks like we're going to."

Then we both just stood there.

No one would make the first move.

It wasn't because we were nervous, it just felt like nothing was there.

It felt very "meh" and awkward.

"We have to, you know," Lena said. "If I want to be alive again like nothing happened."

"Oh, yeah," I said. "Win win for me because you know how bad I want this. Now I can say it was for charity."

"Yeah... you can..."

"Hell yeah."

"Yep."

I looked at the ground and drew an imaginary circle with my toes.

Lena grabbed my hand and placed it on her not-falling-out anymore booby.

I wrote booby just now.

That's how uncomfortable the whole thing was.

"Them's my boobs," she said.

"Yeah, uh," I said. "Feels nice."

"Yeah," Lena said, trying to at least turn on the act to get me in the mood a little. "Feels so good, baby."

"That felt..."

"Yeah, I shouldn't have said that."

She backed up and did a kind of dance. It was like she was trying to strip, but her heart wasn't in it at all. She was just going through the motions. She pushed me down into a chair. She took her bra off and rubbed her... tits?

Then she wrapped her bra around the back of my head. She spun around and pulled my head into her ass.

I choked a little and started coughing.

She sat down and covered herself with a blanket she pulled off my bed.

My laptop and a shit ton of water bottles fell with it.

"You've never cleaned your room a single time in your life, have you?"

"Nope. And you can't make me do it now. Not part of the quest."

"The quest... it was fun while it lasted. Now we have to do... this..."

"Yeah... this..."

"Would it help if I pulled up some videos to get you in the mood?"

"No. My heart just isn't in it anymore."

We sat there for a bit. I played around on my phone, trying to look at pornstars and get in the mood. We had to do this, right? We had to make it, so she never died.

I kept gravitating to women with red hair.

They made me react differently, though.

Their hair was a reminder of something. It was like an emotional switch being flipped back and forth.

Then it hit me.

"Lena," I said. "I'll be back."

She looked at me and raised her hands. The door was closed before she finished saying, "what the fuck?"

It was easy to figure out where I was going. I made a couple calls to a couple of people who I know who I knew would tell me things they weren't technically allowed to.

When I got to where I was going, I knocked frantically. Elsa opened the door. She had cookies and cream ice cream running down her chin and tears coming from her eyes above.

"Well," she said. "How was it?"

"Didn't happen," I said. "I was flaccid the whole time."

I didn't think words could explain any more than that, so I kissed her.

She still had ice cream in her mouth, so it was sort of like making out with the human embodiment of Dairy Queen.

She pulled me inside and we both fell over the arm of her couch. I lay on top of her, and we both started laughing.

Her eyes were glowing.

The first time took like two minutes.

The second time was three.

The third was five.

The fourth only took a minute.

Everything in between took two hours total.

We took a little break after the single minute; I didn't like how I was backtracking and maybe getting worse at this.

We just talked.

It felt odd to me to be lying beside someone and talking about the Dugong while we were naked instead of trying to either go for another round or getting the fuck out of there.

We kept trying to get past ten minutes.

Somewhere around five in the morning, we gave up and slept for a couple hours.

When we woke up, I said, "oh shit, LENA!" and we both got dressed in a hurry.

When we got to my place, she was asleep on my bed. She had my laptop opened beside her looking at pictures of her husband, Ted. What kind of a fucking dweeb is named Ted?

When I picked up the computer, I noticed time had somehow rewound back to the day after Lena's accident.

What the fuck?

Was Mark some kind of time traveler?

Mysteries abound.

"Mmmmmm," she moaned. "I recognize that smell. Is that a hash brown from McDonalds?"

"I thought we could all use some breakfast," I said.

I showed Lena the calendar.

Elsa said it didn't matter.

I wonder now how many times Mark reset time? should we technically be in like year 2897?

Someone needs to keep that guy in check honestly.

Ted showed up a few hours after we decided it was ok for Lena to call him.

She said she left her phone at the airport and missed her layover.

He drove straight from Pennsylvania to southern Ohio in four hours.

When he got there, it was like Lena sensed it. She jumped up and ran outside. Elsa and I looked out the window; luckily, he parked in front of my room so we could see them embrace one another like they had been separated by death.

Maybe something inside Ted told him that had happened?

In the end, I guess I need to find that Miami Dolphins tweet again and thank a couple people.

CHAPTER 14
TIL DEATH OR MARK DO US PART

When you said you wanted us to write our own vows, I didn't know what to do. I scribbled down, "I knew I loved you from the moment I met you."

But that wasn't exactly true.

Then I wrote about how a friend introduced us. That felt too true, but also dishonest in a way.

In the end, I just started writing down those few days we first met.

I don't know who I was doing it for. I think it was to remind myself how far I've come over these past few years.

I'll never forget when you made me wear a graduation cap with a plush dugong sewn to the top.

If I close my eyes, I can see how happy you were when you walked across the stage for your degree in wildlife conservation, not marine biology but close enough.

I can feel the punches in my gut and arms every time I said something obnoxious.

So, here we are.

We're getting married tomorrow.

Lena and Ted Flew in. She had to take a break from filming her new hit. A movie where a guy can only have sex with ghosts; Lena is the star, of course. It's called "Sack-Deep in Ectoplasm."

Shitty title, right?

We didn't do anything when they got here.

No strippers: Lena wanted a night off from that stuff. Who could blame her? And honestly, I didn't feel like dealing with all that, anyway. The small talk is the worst when they first show up.

"Hi, how are you?"

"Good! You?"

"I'm alright."

"Cool! Well, I guess I'll get naked for you now."

I didn't have the energy for all of that.

Ted made nachos, and we played Tetris. Yo, seriously, Ted knows what the fuck he is doing in a kitchen. Lena said, "Ted, get in there and make dinner. Tanner and I are going to sit here and play video games." When he called for us, he had the whole island in the kitchen covered in chips and queso. There was chorizo and grilled chicken all over it, too.

Ted is kind of the shit, if we're being honest.

I'll probably save this thing I've been writing and give it to you on our honeymoon; no one wants me to read an entire book as my vows.

I'll probably just say I really liked your ass or something and make everyone laugh. Just typical bullshit that every dude does when they write their own vows. Lena will probably beat my ass.

Is she my best man or maid of honor?

Mark was here last night to congratulate me.

He said he was going to try to tweak the way he did things a little because apparently his time shit is causing the Mandela Effect. You know, the bear shit or whatever.

I'm kind of dreading the reception. Lena has like five pages of words that are all marked up and drawn on. What it all probably comes down to is that I'm a stupid son of a bitch.

Marty and Melinda were here for a bit. I didn't even look at Melinda's chest once. Lena said she was proud of me. They brought this weird ass wine that tasted like dead leaves and Marty kept saying, "it reflected his soul."

Armand is apparently wearing some weird ass suit to show off his muscles. I don't know why I agreed to let him do the service, or why I agreed to a sock puppet show at the reception.

Whole thing is sort of a fucking mess.

I should close this document and get some sleep. I've got a long day tomorrow.

Make me a promise. When you read this; do not, I repeat, DO NOT summon Mark if I die, as I still believe he's an asshole.

Is that a good enough ending?

I don't think that's a good enough ending.

I probably need to write some sweet and cute little thing here, right?

Fuck it.

Elsa rulz.

ABOUT THE AUTHOR

Damien Casey writes horror comedy. He was made when some guy threw a bunch of b-movie and wrestling vhs tapes in a bonfire. K THX.